Spiny Sea Star

HAPPY READING!

This book is especially for:

_____

Suzanne Tate,
Author—
brings fun and
facts to us in her
Nature Series.

James Melvin,
Illustrator—
brings joyous life
to Suzanne Tate's
characters.

Suzanne and James in costume

Spiny Sea Star

A Tale of Seeing Stars

Suzanne Tate

Illustrated by James Melvin

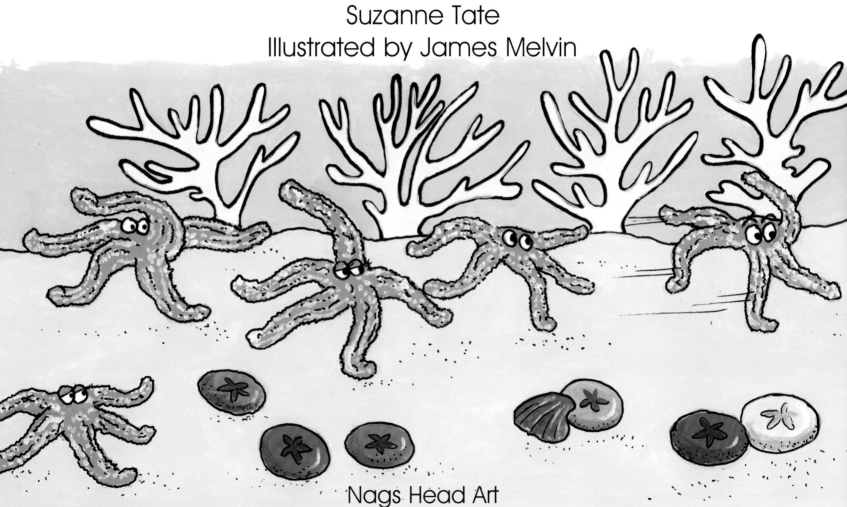

Nags Head Art

To Grandma Grace
who taught us
wonderful lessons of life

Library of Congress Catalog Card Number 2002280399
ISBN 978-1-878405-34-0
ISBN 1-878405-34-9
Published by
Nags Head Art, Inc., P.O. Box 2149, Manteo, NC 27954
Copyright © 2002 by Nags Head Art, Inc.

Spiny Sea Star was a spiny-skinned animal.
He was made up of prickly little plates
that helped him move.

His five arms formed the shape of a star.
Spiny was often called a starfish.
But he wasn't a fish at all!

Spiny had tiny eyes — one at
the end of each arm.
But he didn't have good eyesight
and saw only dark or light.

DARK LIGHT

Thousands of tube feet
lined his spiny arms.
There were little gills in them.

Spiny could breathe through his feet!

The star-shaped creature lived with his family
at the bottom of the sea.
The sea stars could walk along
— one arm at a time!

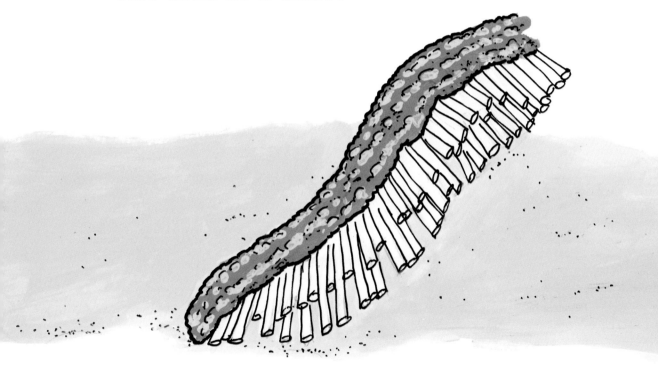

Tiny suction cups on their tube feet
helped them move.

Spiny's brothers and sisters moved slowly so they
could sneak up on clams — a favorite food!
But Spiny pulled himself along the bottom
as fast as he could.

Spiny Sea Star just wanted to be different!
"What fun!" he thought as he made
the sand swirl near a clam bed.

But the clams clammed up and
he couldn't get any meat!

"Spiny, Spiny, can't catch a clammy!"
his brothers and sisters chanted.
They knew that a sea star needs to sneak up
and put its arms around a clam.

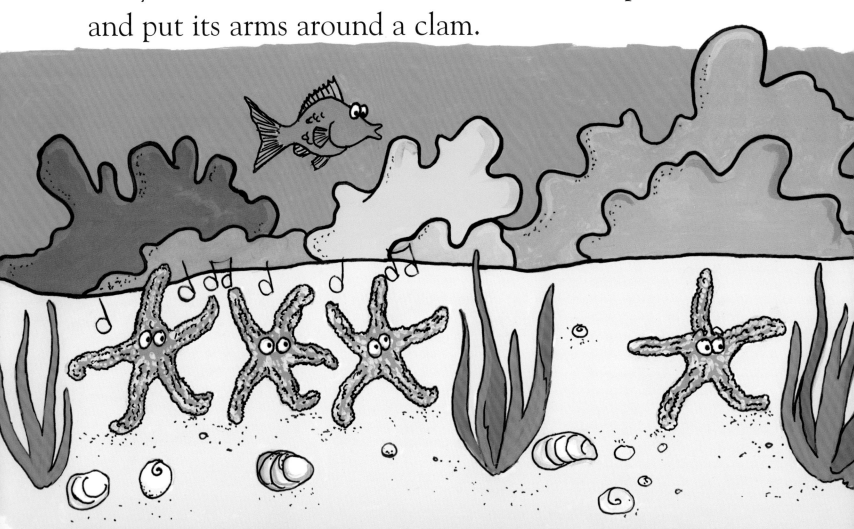

"A sea star must hold on tight," they told Spiny,
"until the clam opens up to breathe.
Then, you can slurp a juicy treat!"

But Spiny didn't take time
to learn from others.

He wondered out loud —

"Why can't I catch a clam?"

A big sea star slowly pulled herself,
— arm after arm — over to his side.

It was Grandma Gracie — the
grandest sea star of all!

"Watch your brothers and sisters," she said.
"See how they take time to catch a clam."

But Spiny just didn't want to listen.
He still rushed around — quickly grabbing
clam after clam.

But the clams clammed up again!

One day, Spiny hurried so fast that
two of his arms tried to go to the left side
— and the other three, to the right!

Grandma Gracie saw him just in time.
"You could break into pieces doing that,"
she warned.

Spiny sank down and pretended
not to listen.

"Let me tell you about your cousin, Silly Sea Star,"
Grandma Gracie said.
"When he was just a little star, he moved
so fast that he broke into five pieces!"

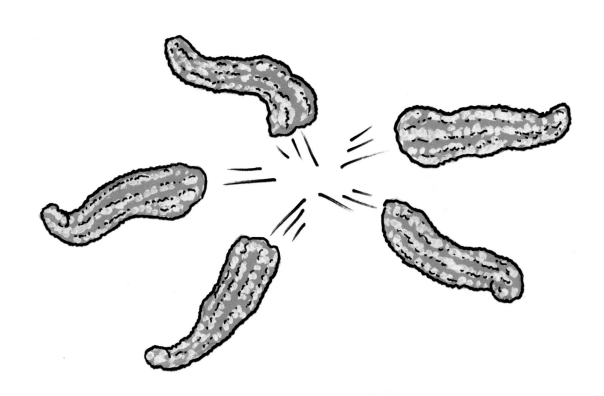

"He grew into five new stars and never was the same again."

But Spiny didn't listen.
"That's just a tall tale!" he said.

One night, Spiny dreamed
about Silly Sea Star.
He saw spiny arms fly off and grow
into five new stars!

Spiny woke up with a start.
Grandma Gracie pulled over to him.
"What is wrong?" she asked.
"I was seeing stars!" he exclaimed.

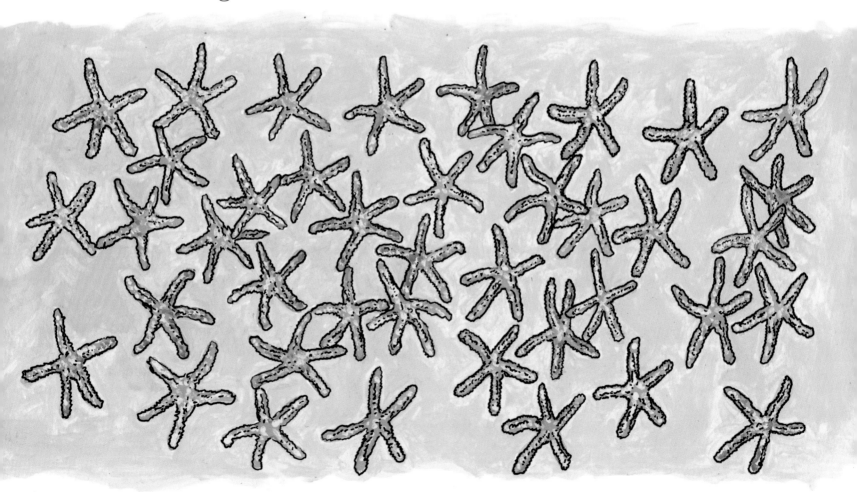

Grandma Gracie listened quietly
as he told her about his dream.
"There is just one thing to do,"
she said. "You must —

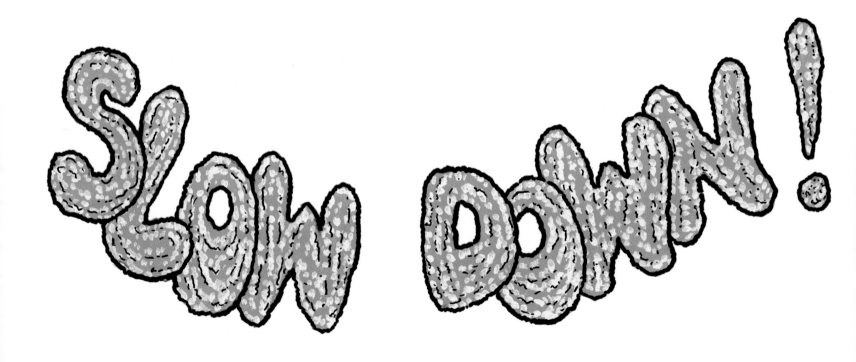

At last, her words began to make sense.
"Maybe I will listen to her!" Spiny thought.

He began to creep arm after arm,
looking for clams.

Spiny sneaked up on a clam and
put his five arms around it.
He waited patiently.

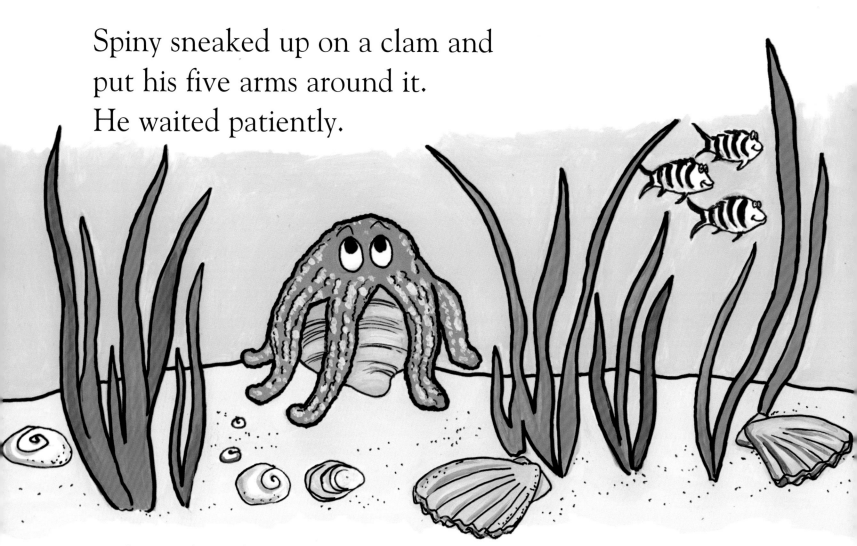

When the clam opened its mouth,
Spiny slurped a tasty treat!

"Grandma Gracie was right,"
he said to himself.
"If you take the time, you can
find many more treats in life."

And ever after, Spiny was
a happy sea star.